BRIGHT EYES, BROWN SKIN

by Cheryl Willis Hudson & Bernette G. Ford

Illustrated by George Ford

Printed in USA

Library of Congress Cataloging in Publication data is available

ISBN: 978-0940975-23-1

http://justusbooks.com

—for our children's children

BRIGHT EYES, BROWN SKIN

**Bright eyes,
Brown skin...**

A heart-shaped face,

A dimpled chin.

Bright eyes,

Cheeks that glow...

Chubby fingers,

Ticklish toes.

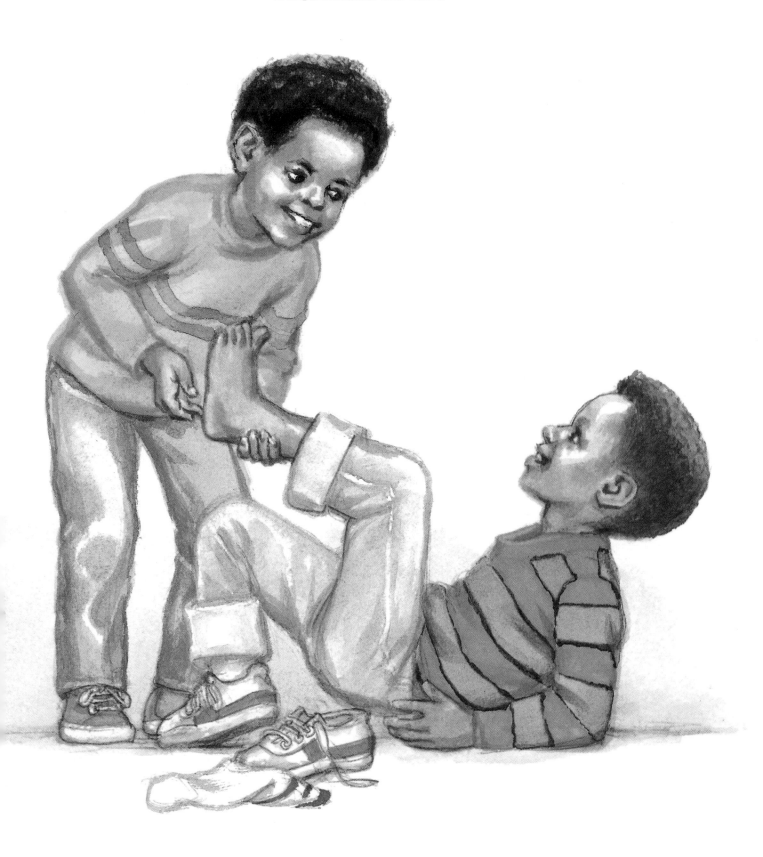

A playful grin,

A perfect nose...

**Very special
Hair and clothes.**

Bright eyes,

Ears to listen...

Lips to kiss you,

Teeth that glisten.

Bright eyes...

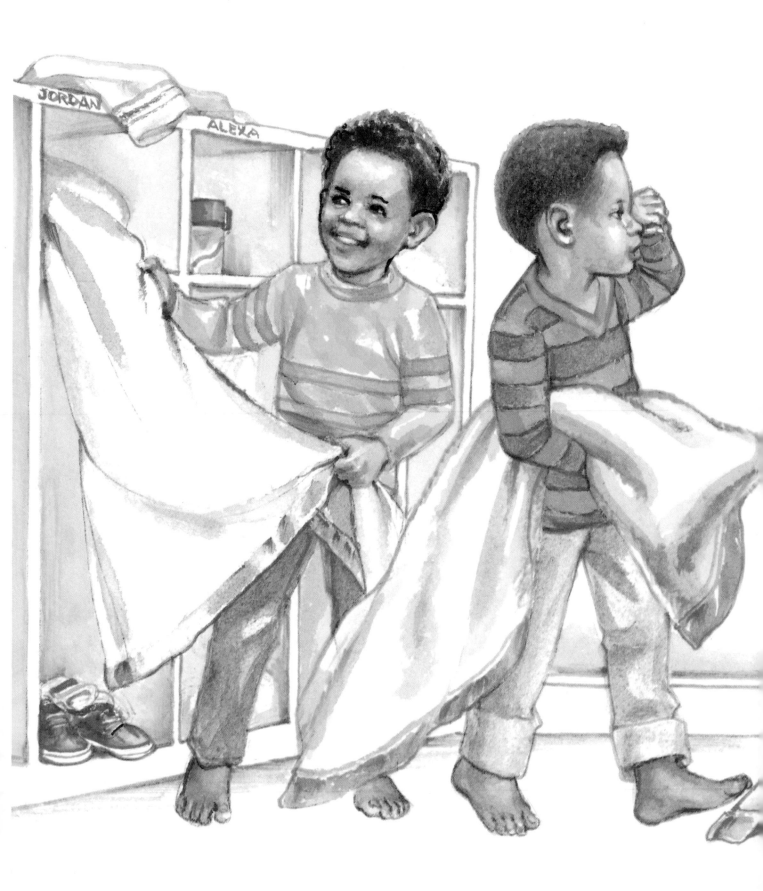

Brown skin...

Warm as toast,

And all tucked in.

Olivia

Jordan

Ethan

Alexa

CHERYL WILLIS HUDSON is an author and graphic designer of children's books. AFRO-BETS® ABC Book and AFRO-BETS® 123 Book were her first published titles and her poems, stories and illustrations for children have appeared in Ebony Jr! and Wee Wisdom Magazine. She has designed many books for major publishing companies, as well.

Ms. Hudson, a native of Portsmouth, Virginia, graduated from Oberlin College in Ohio. She now makes her home in New Jersey with her husband, Wade, and two children, Katura and Stephan.

BERNETTE G. FORD is a publishing executive at a major New York children's book company. Under a pseudonym she has written several books for young readers during the course of her career as an editor. Ms. Ford grew up in Uniondale, New York, and graduated from Connecticut College for Women.

This is the first book on which she and her husband George have collaborated, but it is not the first time their daughter, Olivia, has appeared in George's pictures. Ms. Ford, George and Olivia live in Brooklyn, New York.

GEORGE FORD is a distinguished artist who has illustrated more than two dozen books for young readers. He grew up in the Brownsville and Bedford-Stuyvesant sections of Brooklyn and spent some of his early years on the West Indian island of Barbados. Among the books Mr. Ford has illustrated are AFRO-BETS® First Book About Africa, Muhammad Ali, Far Eastern Beginnings, Paul Robeson, Ego Tripping and Ray Charles, for which he won the American Library Association's Coretta Scott King Award.

You may enjoy other titles published by Just Us Books:

AFRO-BETS® Book of Colors by Margery Wheeler Brown, illustrated by Howard Simpson
AFRO-BETS® Book of Shapes by Margery Wheeler Brown, illustrated by Howard Simpson
AFRO-BETS® Coloring & Activity Book by Dwayne Ferguson
AFRO-BETS® Kids: I'm Gonna Be! by Wade Hudson, illustrated by Culverson Blair
AFRO-BETS® Coloring & Activity Book by Dwayne Ferguson
AFRO-BETS® Quotes for Kids: Words for Kids to Live by Katura J. Hudson, illustrated by Howard Simpson

Annie's Gifts by Angela Medearis, illustrated by Anna Rich
Baby Jesus, Like My Brother by Margery Brown, illustrated by George Ford
Come By Here, Lord: Everyday Prayers for Children by Cheryl Willis Hudson, photos by Monica Morgan
Courtney's Birthday Party by Dr. Loretta Long, illustrated by Ron Garnett
Explore Black History with Wee Pals by Morrie Turner
From a Child's Heart by Nikki Grimes, illustrations by Brenda Joysmith
Glo Goes Shopping by Cheryl Willis Hudson, illustrated by Cathy Johnson
I Told You I Can Play! by Brian Jordan, illustrated by Cornelius Van Wright and Ying-Hwa Hu
Jamal's Busy Day by Wade Hudson, illustrated by George Ford
Kids' Book of Wisdom: Quotes from the Africa American Tradition by Cheryl and Wade Hudson, illustrated by Anna Rich
Land of the Four Winds by Veronica Freeman Ellis, illustrated by Sylvia Walker
MaDear's Old Green House by Denise Lewis Patrick, illustrated by Sonia Lynn Sadler
Many Colors of Mother Goose adapted by Cheryl Willis Hudson
Robo's Favorite Places by Wade Hudson, illustrated by Cathy Johnson
Singing Black: Alternative Nursery Rhymes for Children by Mari Evans, illustrated by Ramon Price
When I Was Little by Toyomi Igus, illustrated by Higgins Bond

Please visit us at www.justusbooks.com